IN THE BEGINNING

Great First Lines from Your Favorite Books

In the Beginning

*Great First Lines from
Your Favorite Books*

Collected by

HANS BAUER

CHRONICLE BOOKS · SAN FRANCISCO

Printed in the United States of America

ISBN 0-8118-0011-3

Library of Congress Cataloging in Publication Data available.

Cover design: Nancy Brescia
Book design: Wilsted & Taylor
Composition: Wilsted & Taylor

Distributed in Canada by Raincoast Books
112 East Third Avenue, Vancouver, B.C. V5T 1C8

10   9   8   7   6   5   4   3   2   1

Chronicle Books
275 Fifth Street
San Francisco, CA 94103

A

You don't know about me without you have read a book by the name of *The Adventures of Tom Sawyer*; but that ain't no matter.

> *The Adventures of Huckleberry Finn*, Mark Twain, 1885

Although she herself was ill enough to justify being in bed had she been a person weak minded enough to give up, Rose Sayer could see that her brother, the Reverend Samuel Sayer, was far more ill.

> *The African Queen*, C. S. Forester, 1935

All true histories contain instruction; though, in some, the treasure may be hard to find, and when found, so trivial in quantity that the dry, shrivelled kernel scarcely compensates for the trouble of cracking the nut.

Agnes Grey, Anne Brontë, 1847

At half-past six on a Friday evening in January, Lincoln International Airport, Illinois, was functioning, though with difficulty.

Airport, Arthur Hailey, 1968

Alice was beginning to get very tired of sitting by her sister on the bank, and having nothing to do: once or twice she had peeped into the book her sister was reading, but it had no pictures or conversations in it, 'and what is the use of a book,' thought Alice, 'without pictures or conversation?'

Alice's Adventures in Wonderland, Lewis Carroll, 1866

We are at rest five miles behind the front.

All Quiet on the Western Front, Erich Maria Remarque, 1928

Strether's first question, when he reached the hotel, was about his friend; yet on his learning that Waymarsh was apparently not to arrive till evening he was not wholly disconcerted.

The Ambassadors, Henry James, 1903

[3]

I met Jack Kennedy in November, 1946.

An American Dream, Norman Mailer, 1965

Dusk—of a summer night.

An American Tragedy, Theodore Dreiser, 1925

As Karl Rossmann, a poor boy of sixteen who had been packed off to America by his parents because a servant girl had seduced him and got herself a child by him, stood on the liner slowly entering the harbour of New York, a sudden burst of sunshine seemed to illumine the Statue of Liberty, so that he saw it in a new light, although he had sighted it long before.

Amerika, Franz Kafka, 1927

Crude thoughts and fierce forces are my state.

Ancient Evenings, Norman Mailer, 1983

The Melekhov farm was right at the end of Tatarsk village.

And Quiet Flows the Don, Mikhail Sholokhov, 1934

Mr. Jones, of the Manor Farm, had locked the hen-houses for the night, but was too drunk to remember to shut the popholes.

Animal Farm, George Orwell, 1946

All happy families are alike but an unhappy family is unhappy after its own fashion.

Anna Karenina, Leo Tolstoy, 1878

The magician's underwear has just been found in a cardboard suitcase floating in a stagnant pond on the outskirts of Miami.

Another Roadside Attraction, Tom Robbins, 1971

Jewel and I come up from the field, following the path in single file.

As I Lay Dying, William Faulkner, 1930

I am not mad, only old.

As We Are Now, May Sarton, 1973

It was the brilliant, high, windless sky of early autumn.

At Heaven's Gate, Robert Penn Warren, 1943

"Who is John Galt?"

Atlas Shrugged, Ayn Rand, 1957

I have been asked to tell you about the back of the North Wind.

At the Back of the North Wind, George MacDonald, 1871

I was born in San Francisco, California.

The Autobiography of Alice B. Toklas, Gertrude Stein, 1933

B

Later that summer, when Mrs. Penmark looked back and remembered, when she was caught up in despair so deep that she knew there was no way out, no solution whatever for the circumstances that encompassed her, it seemed to her that June seventh, the day of the Fern Grammar School picnic, was the day of her last happiness, for never since then had she known contentment or felt peace.

The Bad Seed, William March, 1954

He came into the world in the middle of the thicket, in one of those little, hidden forest glades which seem to be entirely open, but are really screened in on all sides.

Bambi, Felix Salten, 1928

A long sultry Syrian day was drawing near its close.

Barabbas, Marie Corelli, 1893

Since the days of Adam, there has been hardly a mischief done in this world but a woman has been at the bottom of it.

Barry Lyndon, William Thackeray, 1844

The dancers were holding Cee Cee above their heads.

Beaches, Iris Rainer Dart, 1985

We've got a ranch house.

The Beans of Egypt, Maine, Carolyn Chute, 1985

It was a queer, sultry summer, the summer they electro-cuted the Rosenbergs, and I didn't know what I was doing in New York.

The Bell Jar, Sylvia Plath, 1963

The world is what it is; men who are nothing, who allow themselves to become nothing, have no place in it.

A Bend in the River, V. S. Naipaul, 1979

He stood in front of the Tegel Prison gate and was free now.

Berlin Alexanderplatz, Alfred Döblin, 1931

In the beginning God created the heaven and the earth.

The Bible, King James Version, 1611

I first met Pauline Delos at one of those substantial parties Earl Janoth liked to give every two or three months, attended by members of the staff, his personal friends, private moguls, and public nobodies, all in haphazard rotation.

The Big Clock, Kenneth Fearing, 1946

Thundershowers hit just before midnight, drowning out the horn honks and noisemaker blare that usually signalled New Year's on the Strip, bringing 1950 to the West Hollywood Substation in a wave of hot squeals with meat wagon backup.

The Big Nowhere, James Ellroy, 1988

Serena Caudill heard a step outside and then the squeak of the cabin door and knew that John was coming in.

The Big Sky, A. B. Guthrie, Jr., 1947

It was about eleven o'clock in the morning, mid October, with the sun not shining and a look of hard wet rain in the clearness of the foothills.

The Big Sleep, Raymond Chandler, 1939

Martin Daugherty, age fifty and now the scorekeeper, observed it all as Billy Phelan, working on a perfect game, walked with the arrogance of a young, untried eagle toward the ball return, scooped up his black, two-finger ball, tossed it like a juggler from right to left hand, then held it in his left palm, weightlessly.

Billy Phelan's Greatest Game, William Kennedy, 1978

The first place that I can well remember was a large pleasant meadow with a pond of clear water in it.

Black Beauty, Anna Sewell, 1877

The agon, then.

The Black Book, Lawrence Durrell, 1959

I never knew her in life.

The Black Dahlia, James Ellroy, 1987

London.

Bleak House, Charles Dickens, 1853

In that place the wind prevailed.

Bless the Beasts and Children, Glendon Swarthout, 1970

Step, step, step.

Blood in the Rain, Margaret Barbalet, 1986

Having written "The End" to this story of my life, I find it prudent to scamper back here to before the beginning, to my front door, so to speak, and to make this apology to arriving guests: "I promised you an autobiography, but something went wrong in the kitchen."

Bluebeard, Kurt Vonnegut, 1987

At that very moment, in the very sort of Park Avenue co-op apartment that so obsessed the Mayor . . . twelve-foot ceilings . . . two wings, one for the white Anglo-Saxon Protestants who own the place and one for the help . . . Sherman McCoy was kneeling in his front hall trying to put a leash on a dachshund.

The Bonfire of the Vanities, Tom Wolfe, 1987

'David Crimond is here in a *kilt!*'

The Book and the Brotherhood, Iris Murdoch, 1987

Mrs. May lived in two rooms in Kate's parents' house in London; she was, I think, some kind of relation.

The Borrowers, Mary Norton, 1953

The cacophony spun out of control as the crowds swelled through the amusement park in the countryside on the outskirts of Baltimore.

The Bourne Ultimatum, Robert Ludlum, 1990

A squat grey building of only thirty-four stories.

Brave New World, Aldous Huxley, 1932

I am always drawn back to places where I have lived, the houses and their neighborhoods.

Breakfast at Tiffany's, Truman Capote, 1958

This is a tale of a meeting of two lonesome, skinny, fairly old white men on a planet which was dying fast.

Breakfast of Champions, Kurt Vonnegut, 1973

On Friday noon, July the twentieth, 1714, the finest bridge in all Peru broke and precipitated five travellers into the gulf below.

The Bridge of San Luis Rey, Thornton Wilder, 1928

You are not the kind of guy who would be at a place like this at this time of the morning.

Bright Lights, Big City, Jay McInerney, 1984

"And—and—what comes next?"

Buddenbrooks, Thomas Mann, 1902

I've always been a quitter.

Budding Prospects, T. Coraghessan Boyle, 1984

Paint me a small railroad station then, ten minutes before dark.

Bullet Park, John Cheever, 1969

Years ago, a child in a tree with a small caliber rifle bush-whacked a piano through the open summer windows of a neighbor's living room.

The Bushwhacked Piano, Thomas McGuane, 1971

I have noticed that when someone asks for you on the telephone and, finding you out, leaves a message begging you to call him up the moment you come in, and it's important, the matter is more often important to him than to you.

Cakes and Ale, W. Somerset Maugham, 1930

Buck did not read the newspapers, or he would have known that trouble was brewing, not alone for himself, but for every tide-water dog, strong of muscle and with warm, long hair, from Puget Sound to San Diego.

The Call of the Wild, Jack London, 1903

"I've read *many* books," said Professor Mephesto, with an odd finality, wearily flattening his hands on the podium, addressing the seventy-six sophomores who sat in easy reverence, immortalizing his every phrase with their pads and pens, and now, as always, giving him the confidence to slowly, artfully dramatize his words, to pause, shrug, frown, gaze abstractly at the ceiling, allow a wan wistful smile to play at his lips, and repeat quietly, "*many* books . . ."

Candy, Terry Southern and Mason Hoffenberg, 1958

The weather door of the smoking-room had been left open to the North Atlantic fog, as the big liner rolled and lifted, whistling to warn the fishing fleet.

Captains Courageous, Rudyard Kipling, 1897

Daisy's shocked hands met stiff stubble; her breasts were scratched.

Careless Love, Alice Adams, 1967

Nobody was really surprised when it happened, not really, not at the subconscious level where savage things grow.

Carrie, Stephen King, 1974

I opened the window and reached for the puppet head on top of the refrigerator.

A Case of Lone Star, Kinky Friedman, 1987

It was late in the evening when K. arrived.

The Castle, Franz Kafka, 1926

The bitch!

Castle Keep, William Eastlake, 1965

It was love at first sight.

Catch-22, Joseph Heller, 1955

If you really want to hear about it, the first thing you'll probably want to know is where I was born, and what my lousy childhood was like, and how my parents were occupied and all before they had me, and all that David Copperfield kind of crap, but I don't feel like going into it, if you want to know the truth.

The Catcher in the Rye, J.D. Salinger, 1951

Between the marriage elms at the foot of the broad lawn, there hung a scarlet canvas hammock where Andrew Shipley squandered the changeless afternoons of early June.

The Catherine Wheel, Jean Stafford, 1951

"Where's Papa going with that ax?" said Fern to her mother as they were setting the table for breakfast.

Charlotte's Web, E. B. White, 1952

Dad was a tall man, with a large head, jowls, and a Herbert Hoover collar.

Cheaper by the Dozen, Frank B. Gilbreth, Jr., and Ernestine Gilbreth Carey, 1949

For some time now they had been suspicious of him.

Chesapeake, James A. Michener, 1978

For the first fifteen years of our lives, Danny and I lived within five blocks of each other and neither of us knew of the other's existence.

The Chosen, Chaim Potok, 1967

Marley was dead, to begin with, there is no doubt whatever about that.

A Christmas Carol, Charles Dickens, 1843

On the day they were going to kill him, Santiago Nasar got up at five-thirty in the morning to wait for the boat the bishop was coming on.

Chronicle of a Death Foretold, Gabriel García Márquez, 1981

In the *Abalone* (Arizona) *Morning Tribune* for August third there appeared on page five an advertisement eight columns wide and twenty-one inches long.

The Circus of Dr. Laō, Charles G. Finney, 1935

The Prince had all his young life known the story of Sleeping Beauty, cursed to sleep for a hundred years, with her parents, the King and Queen, and all of the Court, after pricking her finger on a spindle.

The Claiming of Sleeping Beauty, A. N. Roquelaure, 1983

"What's it going to be then, eh?"

A Clockwork Orange, Anthony Burgess, 1962

When she was home from her boarding-school I used to see her almost every day sometimes, because their house was right opposite the Town Hall Annexe.

The Collector, John Fowles, 1963

You better not never tell nobody but God.

The Color Purple, Alice Walker, 1982

A green hunting cap squeezed the top of the fleshy balloon of a head.

A Confederacy of Dunces, John Kennedy Toole, 1960

For many years I claimed I could remember things seen at the time of my own birth.

Confessions of a Mask, Yukio Mishima, 1958

It was in Warwick Castle that I came across the curious stranger whom I am going to talk about.

A Connecticut Yankee in King Arthur's Court, Mark Twain, 1889

Pale freckled eggs.

The Conservationist, Nadine Gordimer, 1974

Moscow has grown quiet.

The Cossacks, Leo Tolstoy, 1863

"What did you make of the new couple?"

Couples, John Updike, 1968

Vaughan died yesterday in his last car-crash.

Crash, J. G. Ballard, 1973

Not so long ago, a monster came to the small town of Castle Rock, Maine.

Cujo, Stephen King, 1981

D

AAA CON is the first name in the phone book of most large American cities.

Dad, William Wharton, 1981

It was a diamond all right, shining in the grass half a dozen feet from the blue brick wall.

The Dain Curse, Dashiell Hammett, 1928

You will see, my dear, that I have kept my word and that bonnets and pom-poms do not take up all my time—there will always be some left over for you.

Dangerous Liaisons, Choderlos de Laclos, 1782

The cell door slammed behind Rubashov.

Darkness at Noon, Arthur Koestler, 1941

Somewhere a child began to cry.

Dawn, Elie Wiesel, 1960

Around quitting time, Tod Hackett heard a great din on the road outside his office.

The Day of the Locust, Nathanael West, 1939

When a day that you happen to know is Wednesday starts off by sounding like Sunday, there is something seriously wrong somewhere.

The Day of the Triffids, John Wyndham, 1951

The boy shot Wild Bill's horse at dusk, while Bill was off in the bushes to relieve himself.

Deadwood, Pete Dexter, 1986

For reasons which many persons thought ridiculous,
Mrs. Lightfoot Lee decided to pass the winter in
Washington.

Democracy, Henry Adams, 1880

The light at dawn during those Pacific tests was something to see.

Democracy, Joan Didion, 1984

Yes, I certainly was feeling depressed.

Diary of a Drug Fiend, Aleister Crowley, 1922

An extraordinary thing happened today.

The Diary of a Madman, Nikolai Gogol, 1915

It's the waiting, Shep was thinking.

The Disenchanted, Budd Schulberg, 1950

A merry little surge of electricity piped by automated alarm from the mood organ beside his bed awakened Rick Deckard.

Do Androids Dream of Electric Sheep, Philip K. Dick, 1968

Mr. Utterson the lawyer was a man of a rugged countenance that was never lighted by a smile; cold, scanty and embarrassed in discourse; backward in sentiment; lean, long, dusty, dreary and yet somehow lovable.

Dr. Jekyll and Mr. Hyde, Robert Louis Stevenson, 1886

On they went, singing "Rest Eternal," and whenever they stopped, their feet, the horses, and the gusts of wind seemed to carry on their singing.

Doctor Zhivago, Boris Pasternak, 1957

My wife Norma had run off with Guy Dupree and I was waiting around for the credit card billings to come in so I could see where they had gone.

The Dog of the South, Charles Portis, 1979

At a village of La Mancha, whose name I do not wish to remember, there lived a little while ago one of those gentlemen who are wont to keep a lance in the rack, an old buckler, a lean horse and a swift greyhound.

Don Quixote, Miguel de Cervantes, 1605

I drove out to Glendale to put three new truck drivers on a brewery company bond, and then I remembered this renewal over in Hollywoodland.

Double Indemnity, James M. Cain, 1936

It was the second day of their journey to their first home.

Drums Along the Mohawk, Walter D. Edmonds, 1936

I used to think of him as an ordinary, good-natured, harmless, unremarkable man.

A Dry White Season, André Brink, 1979

In the week before their departure to Arrakis, when all
the final scurrying about had reached a nearly unbearable
frenzy, an old crone came to visit the mother of the boy,
Paul.

Dune, Frank Herbert, 1965

Just as he pulled himself up to the rock-ledge, he heard a sudden rattle, and felt a prick of fangs.

Earth Abides, George R. Stewart, 1949

I sit down, my friend, to comply with thy request.

Edgar Huntly, Charles Brockden Brown, 1799

The lady was extraordinarily naked.

Eight Black Horses, Ed McBain, 1985

"That is New York."

1876, Gore Vidal, 1976

Elmer Gantry was drunk.

Elmer Gantry, Sinclair Lewis, 1927

Wars came early to Shanghai, overtaking each other like the tides that raced up the Yangtze and returned to this gaudy city all the coffins cast adrift from the funeral piers of the Chinese Bund.

Empire of the Sun, J. G. Ballard, 1984

When I was seventeen and in full obedience to my heart's urgent commands, I stepped far from the pathway of normal life and in a moment's time ruined everything I loved—I loved so deeply, and when the love was interrupted, when the incorporeal lady of love shrank back in terror and my own body was locked away, it was hard for others to believe that a life so new could suffer so irrevocably.

Endless Love, Scott Spencer, 1979

In the end is my beginning. . . . That's a quotation I've often heard people say.

Endless Night, Agatha Christie, 1967

Herman Broder turned over and opened one eye.

Enemies, A Love Story, Isaac Bashevis Singer, 1972

That month of June swam into the Two Medicine country.

English Creek, Ivan Doig, 1984

I had the story, bit by bit, from various people, and, as generally happens in such cases, each time it was a different story.

Ethan Frome, Edith Wharton, 1911

In some country towns there exist houses whose appearance weighs as heavily upon the spirits as the gloomiest cloister, the most dismal ruin, or the dreariest stretch of barren land.

Eugénie Grandet, Honoré de Balzac, 1833

Amoebae leave no fossils.

Even Cowgirls Get the Blues, Tom Robbins, 1976

A bankrupt man is a jump ahead of a bankrupt town.

The Executioner Waits, Josephine Herbst, 1934

Brenda was six when she fell out of the apple tree.

The Executioner's Song, Norman Mailer, 1979

Like the brief doomed flare of exploding suns that registers dimly on blind men's eyes, the beginning of the horror passed almost unnoticed; in the shriek of what followed, in fact, was forgotten and perhaps not connected to the horror at all.

The Exorcist, William Peter Blatty, 1971

F

It was a pleasure to burn.

Fahrenheit 451, Ray Bradbury, 1953

During the whole of a dull, dark, and soundless day in the autumn of the year, when the clouds hung oppressively low in the heavens, I had been passing alone, on horseback, through a singularly dreary tract of country; and at length found myself, as the shades of evening drew on, within view of the melancholy House of Usher.

The Fall of the House of Usher (story), Edgar Allan Poe, 1839

It was Friday the thirteenth and yesterday's snowstorm
lingered in the streets like a leftover curse.

Falling Angel, William Hjortsberg, 1978

Slow, law-abiding and drunk, I cruised down North
Main Street toward the river.

Famous All Over Town, Danny Santiago, 1983

Daybreak.

Far Tortuga, Peter Matthiessen, 1975

In the late summer of that year we lived in a house in a village that looked across the river and the plain to the
mountains.

A Farewell to Arms, Ernest Hemingway, 1929

It was one of the mixed blocks over on Central Avenue,
the blocks that are not yet all Negro.

Farewell, My Lovely, Raymond Chandler, 1940

There were 117 psychoanalysts on the Pan Am flight to
Vienna and I'd been treated by at least six of them.

Fear of Flying, Erica Jong, 1973

My lifelong involvement with Mrs. Dempster began at
5:58 o'clock p.m. on the 27th of December, 1908, at
which time I was ten years and seven months old.

Fifth Business, Robertson Davies, 1970

riverrun, past Eve and Adam's, from swerve of shore to bend of bay, brings us by a commodius vicus of recirculation back to Howth Castle and Environs.

Finnegans Wake, James Joyce, 1939

The fretwork hands stood at five past four.

The First Circle, Aleksandr Solzhenitsyn, 1968

The little old kitchen had quieted down from the bustle and confusion of midday, and now, with its afternoon manners on, presented a holiday aspect that, as the principal room in the brown house, it was eminently proper it should have.

Five Little Peppers and How They Grew, Margaret Sidney, 1880

When a journey begins badly it rarely ends well.

The Floating Island, Jules Verne, 1895

Dr. Strauss says I should rite down what I think and remembir and evrey thing that happins to me from now on.

Flowers for Algernon, Daniel Keyes, 1966

Sybil Davison has a genius I.Q. and has been laid by at least six different guys.

Forever . . . , Judy Blume, 1975

That was when I saw the Pendulum.

Foucault's Pendulum, Umberto Eco, 1988

You will rejoice to hear that no disaster has accompanied the commencement of an enterprise which you have regarded with such evil forebodings.

Frankenstein, Mary Shelley, 1816

When he finished packing, he walked out onto the third-floor porch of the barracks brushing the dust from his hands, a very neat and deceptively slim young man in the summer khakis that were still early morning fresh.

From Here to Eternity, James Jones, 1951

Somewhere deep inside the cemetery a bulldozer worked, its drone rising and falling, riding the air like an eagle aboard a thermal.

Gardens of Stone, Nicholas Proffitt, 1983

"When your mama was the geek, my dreamlets," Papa would say, "she made the nipping off of noggins such a crystal mystery that the hens themselves yearned toward her, waltzing around her, hypnotized with longing."

Geek Love, Katherine Dunn, 1983

José Palacios, his oldest servant, found him floating naked with his eyes open in the purifying waters of his bath and thought he had drowned.

> *The General in His Labyrinth,* Gabriel García Márquez, 1989

Everyone knew the party was for someone, but no one quite knew for whom.

> *Get Ready for Battle,* Ruth Prawer Jhabvala, 1962

Bright, clear sky over a plain so wide that the rim of the heavens cut down on it around the entire horizon.

> *Giants in the Earth,* O. E. Rolvaag, 1927

One dollar and eighty-seven cents.

> *The Gift of the Magi* (story), O. Henry, 1906

Today a rare sun of spring.

The Ginger Man, J. P. Donleavy, 1958

"Why does everybody talk about the Virgin Mary?" Suki
asked me.

A Girl of Forty, Herbert Gold, 1986

The night Vincent was shot he saw it coming.

Glitz, Elmore Leonard, 1985

When Joseph Bloch, a construction worker who had
once been a well-known soccer goalie, reported for work
that morning, he was told that he was fired.

The Goalie's Anxiety at the Penalty Kick, Peter Handke, 1970

Amerigo Bonasera sat in New York Criminal Court Number 3 and waited for justice; vengeance on the men who had so cruelly hurt his daughter, who had tried to dishonor her.

The Godfather, Mario Puzo, 1969

Across the street from their house, in an empty lot between two houses, stood the rockpile.

Going to Meet the Man (story), James Baldwin, 1948

The moonlight is falling on to the foot of my bed.

The Golem, Gustav Meyrink, 1915

Scarlett O'Hara was not beautiful, but men seldom realized it when caught by her charm as the Tarleton twins were.

Gone with the Wind, Margaret Mitchell, 1936

It was Wang Lung's marriage day.

The Good Earth, Pearl S. Buck, 1931

This is the saddest story I have ever heard.

The Good Soldier, Ford Madox Ford, 1927

When you are getting on in years (but not ill, of course), you get very sleepy at times, and the hours seem to pass like lazy cattle moving across a landscape.

Goodbye, Mr. Chips, James Hilton, 1934

All nights should be so dark, all winters so warm, all headlights so dazzling.

Gorky Park, Martin Cruz Smith, 1981

A screaming comes across the sky.

Gravity's Rainbow, Thomas Pynchon, 1973

In my younger and more vulnerable years my father gave me some advice that I've been turning over in my mind ever since.

The Great Gatsby, F. Scott Fitzgerald, 1925

There was too much of everything.

Great Son, Edna Ferber, 1944

With the silence and immobility of a great reddish-tinted rock, Thor stood for many minutes looking out over his domain.

The Grizzly King, James Oliver Curwood, 1916

I have had much leisure in the past months to reflect on my first encounter with Fledge, and why he formed such an immediate and intense antipathy toward me.

The Grotesque, Patrick McGrath, 1989

How do people get to this clandestine Archipelago?

The Gulag Archipelago, Aleksandr Solzhenitsyn, 1973

H

It was a small town by a small river and a small lake in a small northern part of a Midwest state.

> *The Halloween Tree,* Ray Bradbury, 1972

We slept in what had once been the gymnasium.

> *The Handmaid's Tale,* Margaret Atwood, 1985

On a bright December morning long ago, two thinly clad children were kneeling upon the bank of a frozen canal in Holland.

> *Hans Brinker or The Silver Skates,* Mary Mapes Dodge, 1865

Now, what I want is Facts.

Hard Times, Charles Dickens, 1854

"Yoh! Ivan. . . . Ivanhoe yoh!"

The Harder They Come, Michael Thelwell, 1980

No live organism can continue for long to exist sanely under conditions of absolute reality; even larks and katy-dids are supposed, by some, to dream.

The Haunting of Hill House, Shirley Jackson, 1959

The *Nellie,* a cruising yawl, swung to her anchor without a flutter of the sails, and was at rest.

Heart of Darkness, Joseph Conrad, 1902

In the town there were two mutes, and they were always together.

The Heart is a Lonely Hunter, Carson McCullers, 1940

The first day I did not think it was funny.

Heartburn, Nora Ephron, 1983

From the pleasantly situated old town of Maienfeld a footpath leads up through shady green meadows to the foot of the mountains, which, as they gaze down on the valley, present a solemn and majestic picture.

Heidi, Johanna Spyri, 1881

What made me take this trip to Africa?

Henderson the Rain King, Saul Bellow, 1959

I was bearing a white phallus through the wood of the world, I was looking for a place to plunge it, a place to surrender it

Her, Lawrence Ferlinghetti, 1960

If I am out of my mind, it's all right with me, thought Moses Herzog.

Herzog, Saul Bellow, 1964

In Paris there are certain streets which are in as much disrepute as any man branded with infamy can be.

History of the Thirteen, Honoré de Balzac, 1883

They put the behemoths in the hold along with the rhinos, the hippos and the elephants.

A History of the World in 10½ Chapters, Julian Barnes, 1989

In a hole in the ground there lived a hobbit.

The Hobbit, J. R. R. Tolkien, 1937

Jack Python walked through the lobby of the Beverly Hills Hotel with every eye upon him.

Hollywood Husbands, Jackie Collins, 1986

The ringing of bells, the surging and swelling of bells supra urbem, above the whole city, in its airs overfilled with sound.

The Holy Sinner, Thomas Mann, 1951

He rolled the cigarette in his lips, liking the taste of the tobacco, squinting his eyes against the sun glare.

Hondo, Louis l'Amour, 1953

I take to pad and pencil, I suppose, because I don't really know what else to do.

Honorable Men, Louis Auchincloss, 1985

Afterwards, in the dusty little corners where London's secret servants drink together, there was argument about where the Dolphin case history should really begin.

The Honourable Schoolboy, John le Carré, 1977

For dessert that night Halmea made a big freezerful of peach ice cream, rich as Jersey milk and thick with hunks of sweet, lockerplant Albertas.

Horseman, Pass By, Larry McMurtry, 1961

On the fifteenth of May, in the jungle of Nool,
In the heat of the day, in the cool of the pool,
He was splashing . . . enjoying the jungle's great joys . . .
When Horton the elephant heard a small noise.

Horton Hears a Who!, Dr. Seuss, 1954

If he had had his way, Peter McDermott thought, he would have fired the chief house detective long ago.

Hotel, Arthur Hailey, 1965

Mr. Sherlock Holmes, who was usually very late in the mornings, save upon those not infrequent occasions when he was up all night, was seated at the breakfast table.

The Hound of the Baskervilles, Sir Arthur Conan Doyle, 1902

Except for her sunglasses, Berry is naked.

The House of God, Samuel Shem, 1978

Halfway down a bystreet of one of our New England towns stands a rusty wooden house, with seven acutely peaked gables, facing towards various points of the compass, and a huge, clustered chimney in the midst.

The House of the Seven Gables, Nathaniel Hawthorne, 1851

"So you boys want to help me on another case?" Fenton Hardy, internationally known detective, smiled at his teen-age sons.

The House on the Cliff/The Hardy Boys, Franklin W. Dixon, 1927

The frowsy chamber-maid of the 'Red Lion' had just finished washing the front door steps.

The House with the Green Shutters, George Douglas Brown, 1901

I am going to pack my two shirts with my other socks and my best suit in the little blue cloth my mother used to tie round her hair when she did the house, and I am going from the Valley.

How Green Was My Valley, Richard Llewellyn, 1940

The little boy named Ulysses Macauley one day stood over the new gopher hole in the backyard of his house on Santa Clara Avenue in Ithaca, California.

The Human Comedy, William Saroyan, 1943

It is three hundred forty-eight years, six months, and nineteen days ago today that the citizens of Paris were awakened by the pealing of all the bells in the triple precincts of the City, the University, and the Town.

The Hunchback of Notre-Dame, Victor Hugo, 1831

Not long ago, there lived in London a young married couple of Dalmatian dogs named Pongo and Missis Pongo.

The Hundred and One Dalmatians, Dodie Smith, 1956

Captain First Rank Marko Ramius of the Soviet Navy was dressed for the Arctic conditions normal to the Northern Fleet submarine base at Polyarny.

The Hunt for Red October, Tom Clancy, 1984

Henry, black and stooped, unlocked the door with a key on a large metal ring.

The Hustler, Walter Tevis, 1959

I shook the rain from my hat and walked into the room.

I, The Jury, Mickey Spillane, 1947

I look at myself in the mirror.

If Beale Street Could Talk (story), James Baldwin, 1974

The village of Holcomb stands on the high wheat plains of western Kansas, a lonesome area that other Kansans call "out there."

In Cold Blood, Truman Capote, 1965

"I have to stop again, hon," Sam's grandmother says, tapping her on the shoulder.

In Country, Bobbie Ann Mason, 1985

At last it was evening.

In Dubious Battle, John Steinbeck, 1936

The strange thing was, he said, how they screamed every night at midnight.

In Our Time (story), Ernest Hemingway, 1925

All beginnings are hard.

In the Beginning, Chaim Potok, 1975

If he is awake early enough the boy sees the men walk past the farmhouse down First Lake Road.

In the Skin of a Lion, Michael Ondaatje, 1987

In watermelon sugar the deeds were done and done again as my life is done in watermelon sugar.

In Watermelon Sugar, Richard Brautigan, 1968

[75]

This journey took place in a part of Canada which lies in the northwestern part of the great sprawling province of Ontario.

The Incredible Journey, Sheila Burnford, 1961

I thought about being dead.

Inferno, Larry Niven and Jerry Pournelle, 1976

That they would come, he had known.

The Institution, Walter Adamson, 1974

"I see . . ." said the vampire thoughtfully, and slowly he walked across the room toward the window.

Interview with the Vampire, Anne Rice, 1976

It was just noon that Sunday morning when the sheriff reached the jail with Lucas Beauchamp though the whole town (the whole county too for that matter) had known since the night before that Lucas had killed a white man.

Intruder in the Dust, William Faulkner, 1948

I warn you that what you're starting to read is full of loose ends and unanswered questions.

Invasion of the Body Snatchers, Jack Finney, 1955

It goes a long way back, some twenty years.

Invisible Man, Ralph Ellison, 1952

The stranger came early in February, one wintry day, through a biting wind and a driving snow, the last snowfall of the year, over the down, walking as it seemed from Bramblehurst railway station, and carrying a little black portmanteau in his thickly gloved hand.

The Invisible Man, H. G. Wells, 1897

Riding up the winding road of Saint Agnes Cemetery in the back of the rattling old truck, Francis Phelan became aware that the dead, even more than the living, settled down in neighborhoods.

Ironweed, William Kennedy, 1983

I do not propose to add anything to what has already been written concerning the loss of the *Lady Vain.*

The Island of Dr. Moreau, H. G. Wells, 1896

I remember the day the Aleut ship came to our island.

Island of the Blue Dolphins, Scott O'Dell, 1960

The terror, which would not end for another twenty-eight years—if it ever did end—began, so far as I know or can tell, with a boat made from a sheet of newspaper floating down a gutter swollen with rain.

It, Stephen King, 1986

How did they meet?

Jacques the Fatalist, Denis Diderot, 1796

There was no possibility of taking a walk that day.

Jane Eyre, Charlotte Brontë, 1847

The great fish moved silently through the night water, propelled by short sweeps of its crescent tail.

Jaws, Peter Benchley, 1973

He wished the phone would stop ringing.

Johnny Got His Gun, Dalton Trumbo, 1939

On rocky islands gulls woke.

Johnny Tremain, Esther Forbes, 1943

It was morning, and the new sun sparkled gold across the ripples of a gentle sea.

Jonathan Livingston Seagull, Richard Bach, 1970

Looking back to all that has occurred to me since that eventful day, I am scarcely able to believe in the reality of my adventures.

A Journey to the Center of the Earth, Jules Verne, 1864

It all began just like that.

The Journey to the End of the Night, Louis-Ferdinand Céline, 1932

The schoolmaster was leaving the village, and everybody seemed sorry.

Jude the Obscure, Thomas Hardy, 1895

It was four o'clock when the ceremony was over and the carriages began to arrive.

The Jungle, Upton Sinclair, 1906

$\mathcal{K}$

She only stopped screaming when she died.

Kane and Abel, Jeffrey Archer, 1979

I will begin the story of my adventures with a certain morning early in the month of June, the year of grace 1751, when I took the key for the last time out of the door of my father's house.

Kidnapped, Robert Louis Stevenson, 1886

He rode into the dark of the woods and dismounted.

The Killer Angels, Michael Shaara, 1974

And so this is what happened.

King Matt the First, Janusz Korczak, 1923

The story begins—when?

The King of the Fields, Isaac Bashevis Singer, 1988

"I'm going to get that bloody bastard if I die in the attempt."

King Rat, James Clavell, 1962

It is a curious thing that at my age—fifty-five last birthday—I should find myself taking up a pen to try and write a history.

King Solomon's Mines, H. Rider Haggard, 1885

—Something a little strange, that's what you notice, that
she's not a woman like all the others.

Kiss of the Spider Woman, Manuel Puig, 1978

He did not expect to see blood.

Kramer versus Kramer, Avery Corman, 1977

Ours is essentially a tragic age, so we refuse to take it tragically.

Lady Chatterley's Lover, D. H. Lawrence, 1928

They sprawled along the counter and on the chairs.

Last Exit to Brooklyn, Hubert Selby, Jr., 1964

One fine day in early summer a young man lay thinking in Central Park.

The Last Gentleman, Walker Percy, 1966

It was a feature peculiar to the colonial wars of North America, that the toils and dangers of the wilderness were to be encountered before the adverse hosts could meet.

The Last of the Mohicans, James Fenimore Cooper, 1826

When I was a young boy, if I was sick or in trouble, or had been beaten at school, I used to remember that on the day I was born my father had wanted to kill me.

The Last of the Wine, Mary Renault, 1956

[87]

Sometimes Sonny felt like he was the only human creature in the town.

The Last Picture Show, Larry McMurtry, 1966

A cool heavenly breeze took possession of him.

The Last Temptation of Christ, Nikos Kazantzakis, 1960

Though I haven't ever been on the screen I was brought up in pictures.

The Last Tycoon, F. Scott Fitzgerald, 1941

Newt Winger lay belly-flat at the edge of the cornfield, his brown chin close to the ground, his eyes glued to a hill of busy ants.

The Learning Tree, Gordon Parks, 1963

It has been a quiet week in Lake Wobegon.

Leaving Home, Garrison Keillor, 1987

Late in October in 1914 three brothers rode from Choteau, Montana, to Calgary in Alberta to enlist in the Great War (the U.S. did not enter until 1917).

Legends of the Fall, Jim Harrison, 1978

"I really don't think he's dead," I said to my three very old friends.

Legs, William Kennedy, 1975

An hour before sunset, on the evening of a day in the beginning of October, a man traveling on foot entered the little town of D——

Les Misérables, Victor Hugo, 1862

People are afraid to merge on freeways in Los Angeles.

Less Than Zero, Bret Easton Ellis, 1985

This was the year he rode the subway to the ends of the city, two hundred miles of track.

Libra, Don DeLillo, 1988

There was a low mist.

Life and Fate, Vasily Grossman, 1980

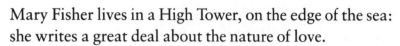

Mary Fisher lives in a High Tower, on the edge of the sea:
she writes a great deal about the nature of love.

The Life and Loves of a She Devil, Fay Weldon, 1983

I wish either my father or my mother, or indeed both of them, as they were in duty both equally bound to it, had minded what they were about when they begot me; had they duly considered how much depended upon what they were then doing;—that not only the production of a rational Being was concerned in it, but that possibly the happy formation and temperature of his body, perhaps his genius and the very cast of his mind;—and, for aught they knew to the contrary, even the fortunes of his whole house might take their turn from the humours and dispositions which were then uppermost;—had they duly weighed and considered all this, and proceeded accordingly,—I am verily persuaded I should have made a quite different figure in the world, from that in which the reader is likely to see me.

The Life and Opinions of Tristram Shandy, Gentleman,

Laurence Sterne, 1760

Sitting beside the road, watching the wagon mount the
hill toward her, Lena thinks, 'I have come from Alabama·
a fur pieon.'

Light in August, William Faulkner, 1932

The boy was about fifteen years old.

The Light in the Forest, Conrad Richter, 1953

I am a white man and never forgot it, but I was brought
up by the Cheyenne Indians from the age of ten.

Little Big Man, Thomas Berger, 1964

Cedric himself knew nothing whatever about it.

Little Lord Fauntleroy, Frances Hodgson Burnett, 1886

'Please, sir, is this Plumfield,' asked a ragged boy of the man who opened the great gate at which the omnibus left him.

Little Men, Louisa May Alcott, 1871

There was once a Chinese boy called Little Pear.

Little Pear, Eleanor Frances Lattimore, 1931

Once when I was six years old I saw a magnificent picture in a book, called *True Stories from Nature,* about the primeval forest.

The Little Prince, Antoine de Saint-Exupéry, 1943

"Christmas won't be Christmas without any presents," grumbled Jo, lying on the rug.

Little Women, Louisa May Alcott, 1868

Lolita, light of my life, fire of my loins.

Lolita, Vladimir Nabokov, 1955

As soon as I got to Borstal they made me a long-distance cross-country runner.

The Loneliness of the Long-Distance Runner, Alan Sillitoe, 1959

The first thing Miss Judith Hearne unpacked in her new lodgings was the silver-framed photograph of her aunt.

The Lonely Passion of Judith Hearne, Brian Moore, 1955

When Augustus came out on the porch the blue pigs were eating a rattlesnake—not a very big one.

Lonesome Dove, Larry McMurtry, 1985

The first time I laid eyes on Terry Lennox he was drunk in a Rolls-Royce Silver Wraith outside the terrace of The Dancers.

The Long Goodbye, Raymond Chandler, 1954

I first saw the light in the city of Boston in the year 1857.

Looking Backward, Edward Bellamy, 1887

Gary Cooper White was born in Jersey City, New Jersey.

Looking for Mr. Goodbar, Judith Rossner, 1975

The boy with fair hair lowered himself down the last few feet of rock and began to pick his way toward the lagoon.

Lord of the Flies, William Golding, 1954

When Mr. Bilbo Baggins of Bag End announced that he would shortly be celebrating his eleventy-first birthday with a party of special magnificence, there was much talk and excitement in Hobbiton.

The Lord of the Rings, Part One—The Fellowship of the Ring,
J. R. R. Tolkien, 1954

Aragorn sped up the hill.

The Lord of the Rings, Part Two—The Two Towers,
J. R. R. Tolkien, 1954

Pippin looked out from the shelter of Gandalf's cloak.
The Lord of the Rings, Part Three—The Return of the King,
J. R. R. Tolkien, 1954

When I crossed the Ashley River my senior year in my gray 1959 Chevrolet, I was returning with confidence and even joy.
The Lords of Discipline, Pat Conroy, 1980

For the following account there are a few minor sources and three major ones; these will be named here at the beginning and not referred to again.
The Lost Honor of Katharina Blum, Heinrich Böll, 1975

Mr. Hungerton, her father, really was the most tactless person upon earth—a fluffy, feathery, untidy cockatoo of a man, perfectly good-natured, but absolutely centred upon his own silly self.

The Lost World, Sir Arthur Conan Doyle, 1912

One day, Annabel saw the sun and moon in the sky at the same time.

Love, Angela Carter, 1971

Now in these dread latter days of the old violent beloved U.S.A. and of the Christ-forgetting Christ-haunted death-dealing Western world I came to myself in a grove of young pines and the question came to me: has it happened at last?

Love in the Ruins, Walker Percy, 1971

It was inevitable: the scent of bitter almonds always
reminded him of the fate of unrequited love.

Love in the Time of Cholera, Gabriel García Márquez, 1985

One day, I was already old, in the entrance of a public
place a man came up to me.

The Lover, Marguerite Duras, 1984

"Monsieur Van Gogh! It's time to wake up!"

Lust for Life, Irving Stone, 1934

M

We were in study hall when the headmaster walked in, followed by a new boy not wearing a school uniform, and by a janitor carrying a large desk.

Madame Bovary, Gustave Flaubert, 1856

All her life, Mrs. Crominski had taken anxiety like a pep-pill.

Madame Sousatzka, Bernice Rubens, 1962

Major Amberson had "made a fortune" in 1873, when other people were losing fortunes, and the magnificence of the Ambersons began then.

The Magnificent Ambersons, Booth Tarkington, 1918

Childhood is a place as well as a time.

The Magnificent Spinster, May Sarton, 1985

I shall soon be quite dead at last in spite of all.

Malone Dies, Samuel Beckett, 1956

Samuel Spade's jaw was long and bony, his chin a jutting
V under the more flexible v of his mouth.

The Maltese Falcon, Dashiell Hammett, 1930

After two miles of walking he came to a town.

The Man Who Fell to Earth, Walter Tevis, 1963

The Law, as quoted, lays down a fair conduct of life, and
one not easy to follow.

The Man Who Would Be King (story), Rudyard Kipling, 1888

The captain never drank.

The Man with the Golden Arm, Nelson Algren, 1949

There was a depression over the Atlantic.

The Man without Qualities Vol. I, Robert Musil, 1930

Should he try to raise the mosquito-netting?

Man's Fate, André Malraux, 1934

All Madrid was astir in the warm summer night, loud with the rumble of lorries stacked with rifles.

Man's Hope, André Malraux, 1938

It was sunny in San Francisco; a fabulous condition.

The Manchurian Candidate, Richard Condon, 1959

The jury said "Guilty" and the Judge said "Life" but he didn't hear them.

The Mansion, William Faulkner, 1959

Every time he drove through Yorkville, Rosenbaum got angry, just on general principles.

Marathon Man, William Goldman, 1974

What is it you think about, Sleeping Beauty, as you ride along the country lanes on that skinny mare of yours?

Marianne, George Sand, 1876

Customs of courtship vary greatly in different times and places, but the way the thing happens to be done here and now always seems the only natural way to do it.

Marjorie Morningstar, Herman Wouk, 1955

It happened that green and crazy summer when Frankie was twelve years old.

The Member of the Wedding, Carson McCullers, 1946

. . . I couldn't seem to find the right room—none of them had the number designated on my pass.

Memoirs Found in a Bathtub, Stanislaw Lem, 1971

If only you could see me now.

Memoirs of an Invisible Man, H. F. Saint, 1987

[106]

She had nothing to fear.

Men and Angels, Mary Gordon, 1985

When Gregor Samsa woke up one morning from unsettling dreams, he found himself changed in his bed into a monstrous vermin.

The Metamorphosis (story), Franz Kafka, 1915

Frederick J. Frenger, Jr., a blithe psychopath from California, asked the flight attendant in first class for another glass of champagne and some writing materials.

Miami Blues, Charles Willeford, 1984

In his new boots, Joe Buck was six-foot-one and life was different.

Midnight Cowboy, James Leo Herlihy, 1965

Many people in the Miracle Valley had theories about why Joe Mondragón did it.

The Milagro Beanfield War, John Nichols, 1974

In the spring of 1931, on a lawn in Glendale, California, a man was bracing trees.

Mildred Pierce, James M. Cain, 1941

It is about water.

Mile Zero, Thomas Sanchez, 1989

Miss Jane Marple was sitting by her window.

The Mirror Crack'd, Agatha Christie, 1962

Often he thought: My life did not begin until I knew her.

Mr. Bridge, Evan S. Connell, 1969

In the spring of 1926 I resigned from my job.

Mr. North, Thornton Wilder, 1973

Her first name was India—she was never able to get used to it.

Mrs. Bridge, Evan S. Connell, 1959

Mrs. Dalloway said she would buy the flowers herself.

Mrs. Dalloway, Virginia Woolf, 1925

Call me Ishmael.

Moby Dick, Herman Melville, 1851

Dr. Sarvis with his bald mottled dome and savage visage, grim and noble as Sibelius, was out night-riding on a routine neighborhood beautification project, burning billboards along the highway—U.S. 66, later to be devoured by the superstate's interstate autobahn.

The Monkey Wrench Gang, Edward Abbey, 1975

I confess that when first I made acquaintance with Charles Strickland I never for a moment discerned that there was in him anything out of the ordinary.

The Moon and Sixpence, W. Somerset Maugham, 1919

We drove past Tiny Polski's mansion house to the main road, and then the five miles into Northampton, Father talking the whole way about savages and the awfulness of America—how it got turned into a dope-taking, door-locking, ulcerated danger zone of rabid scavengers and criminal millionaires and moral sneaks.

The Mosquito Coast, Paul Theroux, 1981

It was five o'clock on a winter's morning in Syria.
Murder on the Orient Express, Agatha Christie, 1934

The autumn of 1803 was one of the finest in the early years of our century, the Napoleonic period.

A Murky Business, Honoré de Balzac, 1841

The sun shone, having no alternative, on the nothing new.

Murphy, Samuel Beckett, 1938

The King having been graciously pleased to comply with a request from the merchants and planters interested in his Majesty's West India possessions, that the bread-fruit tree might be introduced into those islands, a vessel, proper for the undertaking, was bought, and taken into dock at Deptford, to be provided with the necessary fixtures and preparations for executing the object of the voyage.

The Mutiny on the Bounty, William Bligh, 1792

High up on the long hill they called the Saddle Back, behind the ranch and the county road, the boy sat his horse, facing east, his eyes dazzled by the rising sun.

My Friend Flicka, Mary O'Hara, 1941

"Are we rising again?"

The Mysterious Island, Jules Verne, 1874

N

Nobody could sleep.

The Naked and the Dead, Norman Mailer, 1948

I can feel the heat closing in, feel them out there making their moves, setting up their devil doll stool pigeons, crooning over my spoon and dropper I throw away at Washington Square Station, vault a turnstile and two flights down the iron stairs, catch an uptown A train . . .

Naked Lunch, William S. Burroughs, 1959

In the beginning was the Word and the Word was with God, and the Word was God.

The Name of the Rose, Umberto Eco, 1980

Outside the entrance of the Mariabronn cloister, whose rounded arch rested on slim double columns, a chestnut tree stood close to the road.

Narcissus and Goldmund, Hermann Hesse, 1930

Unearthly humps of land curved into the darkening sky like the backs of browsing pigs, like the rumps of elephants.

National Velvet, Enid Bagnold, 1935

The best thing would be to write down events from day to day.

Nausea, Jean-Paul Sartre, 1938

Not the power to remember, but its very opposite, the power to forget, is a necessary condition of our existence.

The Nazarene, Sholem Asch, 1939

The sky above the port was the color of television, tuned to a dead channel.

Neuromancer, William Gibson, 1984

All the beasts in Howling Forest were safe in their caves, nests, and burrows.

The Neverending Story, Michael Ende, 1979

A head of department, working quietly in his room in Whitehall on a summer afternoon, is not accustomed to being disturbed by the nearby and indubitable sound of a revolver shot.

The Nice and the Good, Iris Murdoch, 1968

Stan Carlisle stood well back from the entrance of the canvas enclosure, under the blaze of a naked light bulb, and watched the geek.

Nightmare Alley, William Lindsay Gresham, 1946

The first time we were in bed together he held my hands pinned down above my head.

9½ Weeks, Elizabeth McNeill, 1978

It was a bright cold day in April, and the clocks were striking thirteen.

1984, George Orwell, 1949

You would have to care about the country.

Nobody's Angel, Thomas McGuane, 1979

Six o'clock was striking.

Nocturne, Frank Swinnerton, 1917

I was freezing my ass in the back of the pickup when O. W. Meadows finally turned off the blacktop and pulled to a stop alongside an oat field.

North Dallas Forty, Peter Gent, 1973

No one who had ever seen Catherine Morland in her infancy, would have supposed her born to be an heroine.

Northanger Abbey, Jane Austen, 1818

I am a sick man. . . .

Notes from Underground, Fyodor Dostoevsky, 1864

He left Phoenix in the morning, in the early dawning moments when the world is purple; and he saw, on the highway, banks of spectral birds clustered on the pavement searching for God knows what—certainly not food, not on the bare highway and so near the sleeping city.

Numbers, John Rechy, 1967

One January day, thirty years ago, the little town of Hanover, anchored on a windy Nebraska tableland, was trying not to be blown away.

O Pioneers!, Willa Cather, 1913

A man stood upon a railroad bridge in northern Alabama, looking down into the swift water twenty feet below.

An Occurrence at Owl Creek Bridge, Ambrose Bierce, 1891

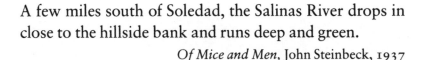

A few miles south of Soledad, the Salinas River drops in close to the hillside bank and runs deep and green.

Of Mice and Men, John Steinbeck, 1937

Now she sits alone and remembers.

The Old Gringo, Carlos Fuentes, 1985

He was an old man who fished alone in a skiff in the Gulf Stream and he had gone eighty-four days now without taking a fish.

The Old Man and the Sea, Ernest Hemingway, 1952

We called him Old Yeller.

Old Yeller, Fred Gipson, 1956

Died on me finally.
Oldest Living Confederate Widow Tells All, Allan Gurganus, 1984

I first met D. an not long after my wife and I split up.
On the Road, Jack Kerouac, 1957

On Mondays, Wednesdays and Fridays it was Court Hand and Summulae Logicales, while the rest of the week it was the Organon, Repetition and Astrology.
The Once and Future King, T. H. White, 1965

Reveille was sounded, as always, at 5 A.M.—a hammer pounding on a rail outside camp HQ.
One Day in the Life of Ivan Denisovich,
Aleksandr Solzhenitsyn, 1962

[125]

They're out there.
One Flew Over the Cuckoo's Nest, Ken Kesey, 1962

Many years later, as he faced the firing squad, Colonel Aureliano Buendía was to remember that distant afternoon when his father took him to discover ice.
One Hundred Years of Solitude, Gabriel García Márquez, 1967

The night in the onion field was a Saturday night.

The Onion Field, Joseph Wambaugh, 1973

To have a reason to get up in the morning, it is necessary to possess a guiding principle.

Ordinary People, Judith Guest, 1976

Last spring, 1846, was a busy season in the city of St. Louis.

The Oregon Trail, Francis Parkman, Jr., 1849

It is not true that a rose by any other name will smell as sweet.

Orley Farm, Anthony Trollope, 1861

How old do you think Mrs. DeGroot really is?

The Other, Thomas Tryon, 1971

I had a farm in Africa, at the foot of the Ngong Hills.

Out of Africa, Isak Dinesen, 1937

When I stepped out into the bright sunlight from the darkness of the movie house, I had only two things on my mind: Paul Newman and a ride home.

The Outsiders, S. E. Hinton, 1967

Gil and I crossed the eastern divide about two by the sun.

The Ox-Bow Incident, Walter Van Tilberg Clark, 1940

P

In the first week of World War II, in the fall of 1939, a six-year-old boy from a large city in central Poland was sent by his parents, like thousands of other children, to the shelter of a distant village.

The Painted Bird, Jerzy Kosinski, 1965

These last few days I have thought and thought of the Nordland summer's endless day.

Pan, Knut Hamsun, 1956

Hell's Kitchen, New York, was probably the hottest place on earth during the summer of '46.

Paradise Alley, Sylvester Stallone, 1977

His feet crunched on the hard-packed sand.

The Pawnbroker, Edward Lewis Wallant, 1961

Kino awakened in the near dark.

The Pearl, John Steinbeck, 1945

In the small hours of a blustery October morning in a south Devon coastal town that seemed to have been deserted by its inhabitants, Magnus Pym got out of his elderly country taxi-cab and, having paid the driver and waited till he had left, struck out across the church square.

A Perfect Spy, John le Carré, 1986

In eighteenth-century France there lived a man who was one of the most gifted and abominable personages in an era that knew no lack of gifted and abominable personages.

Perfume, The Story of a Murderer, Patrick Süskind, 1985

All children, except one, grow up.

Peter Pan, J. M. Barrie, 1911

Indian summer is like a woman.

Peyton Place, Grace Metalious, 1956

There was once a boy named Milo who didn't know what to do with himself—not just sometimes, but always.

The Phantom Tollbooth, Norton Juster, 1961

The studio was filled with the rich odour of roses, and when the light summer wind stirred amidst the trees of the garden there came through the open door the heavy scent of the lilac, or the more delicate perfume of the pink-flowering thorn.

The Picture of Dorian Gray, Oscar Wilde, 1891

I was sick—sick unto death with that long agony; and
when they at length unbound me, and I was permitted to
sit, I felt that my senses were leaving me.

The Pit and the Pendulum (story), Edgar Allan Poe, 1842

The seed bins are empty.

A Place on Earth, Wendell Berry, 1967

What makes Iago evil? some people ask.

Play It as It Lays, Joan Didion, 1970

It was the Sunday after Easter, and the last bull-fight of
the season in Mexico City.

The Plumed Serpent, D. H. Lawrence, 1926

Miss Polly Harrington entered her kitchen a little hurriedly this June morning.

Pollyanna, Eleanor H. Porter, 1913

Well, sir, I should have been sitting pretty, just about as pretty as a man could sit.

Pop. 1280, Jim Thompson, 1964

She was so deeply imbedded in my consciousness that for the first year of school I seem to have believed that each of my teachers was my mother in disguise.

Portnoy's Complaint, Philip Roth, 1969

Under certain circumstances there are few hours in life more agreeable than the hour dedicated to the ceremony known as afternoon tea.

The Portrait of a Lady, Henry James, 1881

Once upon a time and a very good time it was there was a moocow coming down along the road and this moocow that was coming down along the road met a nicens little boy named baby tuckoo. . . .

A Portrait of the Artist as a Young Man, James Joyce, 1916

It began as a mistake.

Post Office, Charles Bukowski, 1971

Maybe I shouldn't have given the guy who pumped my stomach my phone number, but who cares?

Postcards from the Edge, Carrie Fisher, 1987

They threw me off the hay truck about noon.

The Postman Always Rings Twice, James M. Cain, 1934

It is a truth universally acknowledged, that a single man in possession of a good fortune, must be in want of a wife.

Pride and Prejudice, Jane Austen, 1813

In the ancient city of London, on a certain autumn day in the second quarter of the sixteenth century, a boy was born to a poor family of the name of Canty, who did not want him.

The Prince and the Pauper, Mark Twain, 1882

Curdie was the son of Peter the miner.

The Princess and Curdie, George MacDonald, 1882

The year that Buttercup was born, the most beautiful woman in the world was a French scullery maid named Annette.

The Princess Bride, William Goldman, 1973

'I wonder when in the world you're going to do anything, Rudolf?' said my brother's wife.

The Prisoner of Zenda, Anthony Hope, 1894

Norman Bates heard the noise and a shock went through him.

Psycho, Robert Bloch, 1959

The scene of this chronicle is the town of Dawson's Landing, on the Missouri side of the Mississippi, half a day's journey, per steamboat, below St. Louis.

Pudd'nhead Wilson, Mark Twain, 1894

Grimm didn't feel like a clown, but he handed the kid a balloon, anyway.

Quick Change, Jay Cronley, 1981

R

Boys are playing basketball around a telephone pole with a backboard bolted to it.

Rabbit, Run, John Updike, 1960

"Wake up there, youngster," said a rough voice.

Ragged Dick, Horatio Alger, Jr., 1868

In 1902 Father built a house at the crest of Broadview Avenue hill in New Rochelle, New York.

Ragtime, E. L. Doctorow, 1974

They were not railway children to begin with.

The Railway Children, Edith Nesbit, 1960

It looked like a good thing: but wait till I tell you.

The Ransom of Red Chief (story), O. Henry, 1901

It was a chilly evening.

Rashomon, Ryunosuke Akutagawa, 1952

I have never begun a novel with more misgiving.

The Razor's Edge, W. Somerset Maugham, 1944

Last night I dreamt I went to Manderley again.

Rebecca, Daphne du Maurier, 1938

The cold passed reluctantly from the earth, and the retiring fogs revealed an army stretched out on the hills, resting.

The Red Badge of Courage, Stephen Crane, 1895

At daybreak Billy Buck emerged from the bunkhouse and stood for a moment on the porch looking up at the sky.

The Red Pony, John Steinbeck, 1937

We were using the old blue china and the stainless steel cutlery, with place mats on the big oval table and odd-sized jelly glasses for the wine.

Red Sky at Morning, Richard Bradford, 1968

For a long time I used to go to bed early.

Remembrance of Things Past, Volume 1, Swann's Way,
Marcel Proust, 1913

The story so far:
In the beginning the Universe was created.

The Restaurant at the End of the Universe, Douglas Adams, 1980

You could not tell if you were a bird descending (and there was a bird descending, a vulture) if the naked man was dead or alive.

Revenge, Jim Harrison, 1978

Click.

Ride with Me, Mariah Montana, Ivan Doig, 1990

A sharp clip-clop of iron-shod hoofs deadened and died away, and clouds of yellow dust drifted from under the cottonwoods out over the sage.

Riders of the Purple Sage, Zane Grey, 1912

In our family, there was no clear line between religion and fly fishing.

A River Runs Through It, Norman Maclean, 1976

Because she was only fifteen and busy with her growing up, Lucia's periods of reflection were brief and infrequent; but this morning she felt weighted with responsibility.

The Robe, Lloyd C. Douglas, 1942

At five o'clock in the afternoon, which was late in March, the stainless blue of the sky over Rome had begun to pale and the blue transparency of the narrow streets had gathered a faint opacity of vapor.

The Roman Spring of Mrs. Stone, Tennessee Williams, 1950

"The Signora had no business to do it," said Miss Bart-
lett, "no business at all."

A Room with a View, E. M. Forster, 1908

Early in the spring of 1750, in the village of Juffure, four
days upriver from the coast of The Gambia, West Africa,
a manchild was born to Omoro and Binta Kinte.

Roots, Alex Haley, 1976

No one remembers her beginnings.

Rubyfruit Jungle, Rita Mae Brown, 1973

Lily heard the shot at seventeen minutes to one.

Run River, Joan Didion, 1963

'To be born again,' sang Gibreel Farishta tumbling from the heavens, 'first you have to die.'

The Satanic Verses, Salman Rushdie, 1988

He was born with a gift of laughter and a sense that the world was mad.

Scaramouche, Rafael Sabatini, 1921

In Beverly Hills only the infirm and the senile do not drive their own cars.

Scruples, Judith Krantz, 1978

Night was running ahead of itself.

Sea of Death, Jorge Amado, 1984

Often January brings a strange false spring to much of northern California.

Second Chances, Alice Adams, 1988

The sun reverberated off the buildings with the brilliance of a handful of diamonds cast against an iceberg, the shimmering white was blinding, as Sabina lay naked on a deck chair in the heat of the Los Angeles sun.

Secrets, Danielle Steel, 1985

When it came to concealing his troubles, Tommy Wilhelm was not less capable than the next fellow.

Seize the Day, Saul Bellow, 1956

I went back to the Devon School not long ago, and found it looking oddly newer than when I was a student there fifteen years before.

A Separate Peace, John Knowles, 1960

He rode into our valley in the summer of '89.

Shane, Jack Schaefer, 1949

There are some events of which each circumstance and surrounding detail seem to be graven on the memory in such fashion that we cannot forget them.

She, H. Rider Haggard, 1976

He awoke, opened his eyes.

The Sheltering Sky, Paul Bowles, 1949

August, 1931—The port town of Veracruz is a little purgatory between land and sea for the traveler, but the people who live there are very fond of themselves and the town they have helped to make.

Ship of Fools, Katherine Anne Porter, 1945

My father said he saw him years later playing in a tenth-rate commercial league in a textile town in Carolina, wearing shoes and an assumed name.

Shoeless Joe, W. P. Kinsella, 1982

In the shade of the house, in the sunshine on the river bank by the boats, in the shade of the sallow wood and the fig tree, Siddhartha, the handsome Brahmin's son, grew up with his friend Govinda.

Siddhartha, Hermann Hesse, 1951

Sherlock Holmes took his bottle from the corner of the mantel-piece and his hypodermic syringe from its neat morocco case.

The Sign of the Four, Sir Arthur Conan Doyle, 1889

Waking up begins with saying *am* and *now.*

A Single Man, Christopher Isherwood, 1964

All this happened, more or less.

Slaughterhouse-Five, Kurt Vonnegut, 1968

A single bird call began the day.

The Slave, Isaac Bashevis Singer, 1962

After I became a prostitute, I had to deal with penises of every imaginable shape and size.

Slaves of New York, Tama Janowitz, 1986

Two seemingly unconnected events heralded the summons of Mr. George Smiley from his dubious retirement.

Smiley's People, John le Carré, 1979

You walk down the street at night.

The Snake, Mickey Spillane, 1964

I thought that going to high school was going to be a big improvement over what I was used to.

The Snarkout Boys and the Avocado of Death,
Daniel Pinkwater, 1982

The moon rises.

The Snarkout Boys and the Baconburg Horror,
Daniel Pinkwater, 1984

"The marvellous thing is that it's painless," he said.

The Snows of Kilimanjaro (story), Ernest Hemingway, 1961

"Mister Deck, are you my stinkin' Daddy?" a youthful, female, furious voice said into the phone.

Some Can Whistle, Larry McMurtry, 1989

I get the willies when I see closed doors.
Something Happened, Joseph Heller, 1974

First of all, it was October, a rare month for boys.
Something Wicked This Way Comes, Ray Bradbury, 1962

To Sparrow, her father was a man standing in front of a Day-Glo green VW van in a picture dated June 1969.
Somewhere off the Coast of Maine, Ann Hood, 1987

In those days cheap apartments were almost impossible to find in Manhattan, so I had to move to Brooklyn.
Sophie's Choice, William Styron, 1979

How happy I am to have come away!

The Sorrows of Young Werther, Johann Wolfgang von Goethe, 1774

The tall man stood at the edge of the porch.

Sounder, William H. Armstrong, 1969

A sky as pure as water bathed the stars and brought them out.

Southern Mail, Antoine de Saint-Exupéry, 1929

On 24 October 1944 planet earth was following its orbit about the sun as it has obediently done for nearly five billion years.

Space, James A. Michener, 1982

All my life I have had an awareness of other times and places.

The Star Rover, Jack London, 1914

Laurel was thirteen years old.

Stella Dallas, Olive Higgins Prouty, 1923

The day had gone by just as days go by.

Steppenwolf, Hermann Hesse, 1929

Once upon a time, many years ago—when our grand-fathers were little children—there was a doctor, and his name was Dolittle—John Dolittle, M.D.

The Story of Doctor Dolittle, Hugh Lofting, 1920

Her lover one day takes O for a walk in a section of the city where they never go—the Montsouris Park, the Monceau Park.

Story of O, Pauline Réage, 1954

Maman died today.

The Stranger, Albert Camus, 1942

Once upon a time there was a Martian named Valentine Michael Smith.

Stranger in a Strange Land, Robert A. Heinlein, 1961

He sat perfectly still in front of the television set in room 932 of the Biltmore Hotel.

A Stranger Is Watching, Mary Higgins Clark, 1977

For many days we had been tempest-tossed.

The Swiss Family Robinson, Johann Wyss, 1814

T

It was the best of times, it was the worst of times, it was the age of wisdom, it was the age of foolishness, it was the epoch of belief, it was the epoch of incredulity, it was the season of Light, it was the season of Darkness, it was the spring of hope, it was the winter of despair, we had everything before us, we had nothing before us, we were all going direct to Heaven, we were all going direct the other way—in short, the period was so far like the present period, that some of its noisiest authorities insisted on its being received, for good or for evil, in the superlative degree of comparison only.

A Tale of Two Cities, Charles Dickens, 1859

He believed he was safe.

Tar Baby, Toni Morrison, 1981

I had this story from one who had no business to tell it to me, or to any other.

Tarzan of the Apes, Edgar Rice Burroughs, 1914

My notes on my first session with don Juan are dated June 23, 1961.

The Teachings of Don Juan: A Yaqui Way of Knowledge,
Carlos Castaneda, 1968

True!—nervous—very, very dreadfully nervous I had been and am; but why *will* you say that I am mad?

The Tell-Tale Heart (story), Edgar Allan Poe, 1843

[165]

There is an old legend that somewhere in the world every man has his double.

The Tenth Man, Graham Greene, 1985

I was leaning against a bar in a speakeasy on Fifty-second Street, waiting for Nora to finish her Christmas shopping, when a girl got up from the table where she had been sitting with three other people and came over to me.

The Thin Man, Dashiell Hammett, 1933

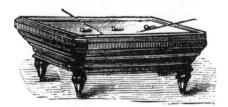

It was one of those days when it seemed to James Bond that all life, as someone put it, was nothing but a heap of six to four against.

Thunderball, Ian Fleming, 1961

In shirt-sleeves, the way I generally worked, I sat sketching a bar of soap taped to an upper corner of my drawing board.

Time and Again, Jack Finney, 1970

The time traveller (for so it will be convenient to speak of him) was expounding a recondite matter to us.

The Time Machine, H. G. Wells, 1895

Granted: I am an inmate of a mental hospital; my keeper is watching me, he never lets me out of his sight; there's a peephole in the door, and my keeper's eye is the shade of brown that can never see through a blue-eyed type like me.

The Tin Drum, Günter Grass, 1959

You know how it is there early in the morning in Havana with the bums still asleep against the walls of the buildings; before even the ice wagons come by with ice for the bars?

To Have and Have Not, Ernest Hemingway, 1937

When he was nearly thirteen, my brother Jem got his arm badly broken at the elbow.

To Kill a Mockingbird, Harper Lee, 1960

"Yes, of course, if it's fine tomorrow," said Mrs. Ramsay.

To the Lighthouse, Virginia Woolf, 1927

Lov Bensey trudged homeward through the deep white sand of the gully-washed tobacco road with a sack of winter turnips on his back.

Tobacco Road, Erskine Caldwell, 1932

"Couldn't you give more 'n six peanuts for a cent?" was a question asked by a very small boy, with big, staring eyes, of a candy vendor at a circus booth.

Toby Tyler, James Otis, 1881

For want of a nail the kingdom was lost—that's how the catechism goes when you boil it down.

The Tommyknockers, Stephen King, 1987

When Danny came home from the army he learned that he was an heir and an owner of property.

Tortilla Flat, John Steinbeck, 1935

We started dying before the snow, and like the snow, we continued to fall.

Tracks, Louise Erdrich, 1988

Squire Trelawney, Dr. Livesey, and the rest of these gentlemen having asked me to write down the whole particulars about Treasure Island, from the beginning to the end, keeping nothing back but the bearings of the island, and that only because there is treasure still not yet lifted, I take up my pen in the year of grace 17__, and go back to the time when my father kept the Admiral Benbow Inn, and the brown old seaman, with the saber cut, first took up his lodging under our roof.

Treasure Island, Robert Louis Stevenson, 1883

The bench on which Dobbs was sitting was not so good.

The Treasure of the Sierra Madre, B. Traven, 1935

Serene was a word you could put to Brooklyn, New York.

A Tree Grows in Brooklyn, Betty Smith, 1943

I am living at the Villa Borghese.

Tropic of Cancer, Henry Miller, 1934

When Harold was three or four, his father and mother took him to a swimming pool.

Trust Me, John Updike, 1962

The year 1866 was signalised by a remarkable incident, a mysterious and puzzling phenomenon, which doubtless no one has yet forgotten.

20,000 Leagues Under the Sea, Jules Verne, 1869

The drought had lasted now for ten million years, and the reign of the terrible lizards had long since ended.

2001 A Space Odyssey, Arthur C. Clarke, 1968

U

Stately, plump Buck Mulligan came from the stairhead, bearing a bowl of lather on which a mirror and a razor lay crossed.

Ulysses, James Joyce, 1934

The idea of eternal return is a mysterious one, and Nietzsche has often perplexed other philosophers with it: to think that everything recurs as we once experienced it, and that the recurrence itself recurs ad infinitum!

The Unbearable Lightness of Being, Milan Kundera, 1984

Late in the afternoon of a chilly day in February, two gentlemen were sitting alone over their wine, in a well-furnished dining parlor, in the town of P———, in Kentucky.

Uncle Tom's Cabin, Harriet Beecher Stowe, 1852

I've always been a liar—it runs in my family.

Utrillo's Mother, Sarah Baylis, 1987

V

She was dead.

The Valley of Horses, Jean M. Auel, 1982

There was once a velveteen rabbit, and in the beginning
he was really splendid.

The Velveteen Rabbit, Margery Williams, 1922

The guy was dead as hell.

Vengeance Is Mine!, Mickey Spillane, 1950

I was ever of opinion, that the honest man who married and brought up a large family, did more service than he who continued single, and only talked of population.

The Vicar of Wakefield, Oliver Goldsmith, 1766

On some nights New York is as hot as Bangkok.

The Victim, Saul Bellow, 1947

Some notable sight was drawing the passengers, both men and women, to the window; and therefore I rose and crossed the car to see what it was.

The Virginian, Owen Wister, 1902

She hasn't been dead four months and I've already eaten
to the bottom of the deep freeze.

A Virtuous Woman, Kaye Gibbons, 1989

It was as if no one had heard.

The Voyeur, Alain Robbe-Grillet, 1958

W

'Eh bien, mon prince, so Genoa and Lucca are now no more than family estates of the Bonapartes.'

War and Peace, Leo Tolstoy, 1869

Seven years came and went.

Warlock, Jim Harrison, 1981

The primroses were over.

Watership Down, Richard Adams, 1972

Mr. Hackett turned the corner and saw, in the failing light, at some little distance, his seat.

Watt, Samuel Beckett, 1953

Petrograd smelt of carbolic acid.

We the Living, Ayn Rand, 1936

Nothing ever begins.

Weaveworld, Clive Barker, 1987

The old writer lived in a boxcar by the river.

The Western Lands, William S. Burroughs, 1987

"The book must be dropped."

What's Bred in the Bone, Robertson Davies, 1985

When I left my office that beautiful spring day, I had no idea what was in store for me.

Where the Red Fern Grows, Wilson Rawls, 1961

When I think back now, I realize that the only thing John Wilson and I actually ever had in common was the fact that at one time or another each of us ran over someone with an automobile.

White Hunter, Black Heart, Paul Viertel, 1953

She entered, as Venus from the sea, dripping.
White Mule, William Carlos Williams, 1937

Lula and her friend Beany Thorn sat at a table in the Raindrop Club drinking rum Co-Colas while watching and listening to a white blues band called The Bleach Boys.
Wild at Heart, Barry Gifford, 1990

The Mole had been working very hard all the morning, spring-cleaning his little home.
The Wind in the Willows, Kenneth Grahame, 1908

[182]

Here is Edward Bear, coming downstairs now, bump, bump, bump, on the back of his head, behind Christopher Robin.

Winnie-the-Pooh, A. A. Milne, 1926

Hazel Motes sat at a forward angle on the green plush train seat, looking one minute at the window as if he might want to jump out of it, and the next down the aisle at the other end of the car.

Wise Blood, Flannery O'Connor, 1952

The island of Gont, a single mountain that lifts its peak a mile above the storm-racked Northeast Sea, is a land famous for wizards.

A Wizard of Earthsea, Ursula K. Le Guin, 1968

Has my watch stopped?

The Woman Destroyed, Simone de Beauvoir, 1967

One day in August a man disappeared.

The Woman in the Dunes, Kobo Abé, 1964

This is the story of what a Woman's patience can endure,
and what a Man's resolution can achieve.

The Woman in White, Wilkie Collins, 1860

I was 50 years old and hadn't been to bed with a woman
for four years.

Women, Charles Bukowski, 1978

The rattling moving van crept up Brewster like a huge
green slug.

The Women of Brewster Place, Gloria Naylor, 1982

Mira was hiding in the ladies' room.

The Women's Room, Marilyn French, 1977

Dorothy lived in the midst of the great Kansas prairies, with Uncle Henry, who was a farmer, and Aunt Em, who was the farmer's wife.

The Wonderful Wizard of Oz, L. Frank Baum, 1900

Garp's mother, Jenny Fields, was arrested in Boston in 1942 for wounding a man in a movie theater.

The World According to Garp, John Irving, 1978

Children are like jam: all very well in the proper place, but you can't stand them all over the shop—eh, what?
The Wouldbegoods, Edith Nesbit, 1901

It was a dark and stormy night.
A Wrinkle in Time, Madeleine L'Engle, 1962

There's no accounting for laws.
The Wrong Case, James Crumley, 1975

1801—I have just returned from a visit to my landlord— the solitary neighbour that I shall be troubled with.
Wuthering Heights, Emily Brontë, 1847

X

In May 1979, only days after Britains knew conservative government came to power, the yellow box that contains the daily report from MI6 to the Prime Minister was delivered to her by a deputy secretary in the Cabinet Office.

XPD, Len Deighton, 1981

Y

A column of smoke rose thin and straight from the cabin chimney.

The Yearling, Marjorie Kinnan Rawlings, 1938

It was the hour of twilight on a soft spring day toward the end of April in the year of Our Lord 1929, and George Webber leaned his elbows on the sill of his back window and looked out at what he could see of New York.

You Can't Go Home Again, Thomas Wolfe, 1934

Not once upon a time but a few years ago.

You Must Remember This, Joyce Carol Oates, 1987

The Geisha called "Trembling Leaf," on her knees beside James Bond, leant forward from the waist and kissed him chastely on the right cheek.

You Only Live Twice, Ian Fleming, 1964

Have you ever known a famous man before he became famous?

Youngblood Hawke, Herman Wouk, 1962

I first met him in Piraeus.

Zorba the Greek, Nikos Kazantzakis, 1952

INDEX